Proudly presented to:
Erin Colleen

From: *Love,*
Grammie & Poppie

Date:
Christmas
2001

Text by Mark Kimball Moulton
Illustrated by Karen Hillard Crouch
© Copyright 2000. All rights reserved.
Printed in the U.S.A.

Published by Lang Books
A Division of R.A. Lang Card Company, Ltd.
514 Wells Street · Delafield, WI 53018
262.646.2211 · www.lang.com

ISBN:0-7412-0439-8
10 9 8 7 6 5 4 3 2 1
second edition

Other books to collect
By Storyteller Mark Kimball Moulton:

A Snowman Named Just Bob
Everyday Angels
Caleb's Lighthouse
A Cricket's Carol
Reindeer Moon
The Night at Humpback Bridge

This story was inspired by
all of you who know in your heart
that it's not who you love that matters,
but that you love and are loved.
I dedicate this story to my loving Mom
and Aunt Fran, Debbie, Missy, Lane,
and of course, my own special
sweetheart, "Queenie."

mkm

'Ditto' what Mark said.
Love is a beautiful thing.
Especially for my dear sister Becky,
who always had an appreciation
for little critters
(she even lassoed a
racoon once, it's true!).
and to 'Sir', with Love.

Happy wishes to Logan Orion
and Lee Wilder...

Grams

KHC

One Enchanted Evening

Written by
Mark Kimball Moulton

Art by
Karen Hillard Crouch

Lang Books
Delafield, WI

"right this way..."

Not far away, just beyond the sunrise,
is a land ruled by spiders
and blue bottleflies

Where mosquitoes laugh
and dragonflies giggle
at jokes told by turtles
and worms as they wiggle. . .

. . .A wonderful place filled with
beauty and grace,
where life is lived slowly,
just at a snails pace.

"Knock,
knock..."

So open the window
and follow your dreams,

out through the brown fields,
down the path by the stream.

Find a comfortable seat lit by a moonbeam,
and hear this tale of Fieldmouse
and his beloved Queen.

(It's a tale of the most enchanting romance
that began at the Annual Mid-Summer's Eve Dance. . .)

Dear Queen Spider was sitting and weaving her web when Sir Fieldmouse came upon her, he bowed and he said...

"Time has come, my dear Queen, for your work to be done. You've toiled all the day and your web's nearly spun.

May I ask you to join me in a dance, just for fun?"

Well, Queen Spider, she stuttered, she blushed and she cried,
for a date with Sir Fieldmouse, _any_ girl would have died!

"Why yes, my good Fieldmouse,
I'd <u>love</u> to attend and dance 'til my
eight legs will no longer bend!

After all, it is evening and
my work should now end — but
you must call me "Queenie",
if we're to be friends!"

So the Royal Flea-Maidens helped
Queenie to don a most beautiful
gown of soft, pink chiffon.

Fieldmouse brought gardenias and
chocolate Bon-Bons. He looked oh,
so regal with his tuxedo on!

They enlisted a firefly and flew to the
ball — Queen Spider held tight
so neither would fall!

They arrived with a flourish, long
before curtain call, and they bowed
and they curtsied to one and to all.

Welcome to the Midsummer's Eve Dance

They made quite the entrance,
their friends were so pleased.
"What have we here, a new couple?,"
they teased.

But Queenie and Mouse
paid no attention to these.

This enchanting affair
was held on the banks
of Swan Lake.

There were cattails
with candles and
a juicy clambake,

and dandelion puffs that
blew through the air
with each shake,

and drinks chilled
with little
tiny snowflakes,

and at midnight
they served
the most
magnificent cake!

hm...hm...hm ♪

The orchestra
struck up a soft "Pastorale,"
then crooned out a love song
called "Me and My Gal."
Cricket played the viola,
Moth her violin,
Toad croaked out
the chorus,
Tree Frog joined right in!
Madam Bee of the Bumble
hummed a beautiful tune
and a romantic ballad
was sung by Miss Loon.

♪♪ "Feelings..."

The First Lady Bug flirted
and batted her eyes at the
handsome Little Lord Blue Bottlefly.

That he flirted back was no big
surprise for the First Lady's
beauty was known
far and wide!

"Oh! my
Beloved
Lady..."

Love Poems

Butterfly had arrived from the Castle Cocoon —
she was recently back from her honeymoon.

She flew on the dance floor with great finesse
and she swirled and she twirled in her brand new dress!

Caterpillar sailed in on a leaf for his boat
to show off his brand new striped winter coat.
He hadn't a penny to pay for his meal
so he did a tap dance that made everyone squeal!

Reverend Mantis was praying and said just a word
'bout the dee-licious dinner that soon would be served.

There was dandelion salad and roast chestnut pate'
and in honor of Queenie, bowls of fresh curds and whey.

By eleven the party was still
going quite strong.

Queenie and Sir Fieldmouse
had danced every song and
Queen Spiders eight legs had kept
up all night long!

They dazzled the crowd, they made quite the
pair, with the moon in their eyes and starlight in their hair.

Soon Queenie was smitten and Sir Fieldmouse, in love.
Their friends were so happy that's all they talked of!

Now, you'll never believe
what has happened since then.
Queen Spider and Sir Fieldmouse
have become <u>more</u> than friends!

They've married and everything's
worked out just right, though she weaves
in the daytime and he works late at night.

Some say it's peculiar, a most unusual sight,
her being Queen Spider...
Fieldmouse just a knight.

"We're gonna
be
late!"

But true love can be funny,
a most curious thing.

You just never know who
(or what) will make your heart sing

and why question the
happiness true love doth bring?

But still <u>why</u>, you might ask,
would a <u>mouse</u> love a <u>bug</u>?

Just think of Queenie's
eight legs and how she must hug!

And though they are different
in station and form,

their lives are just perfect,
though far from the norm.

So if you're wishing for true love,
what's important, it seems...

"Here's
to Love."

is to accept

all the differences...

and to share

the same dreams.

The End
...Adieu